T0153433

THE
HAUNTED BOOKSHELF

The telling or reading of ghost stories during long, dark, and cold Christmas nights is a yuletide ritual dating back to at least the eighteenth century, and was once as much a part of Christmas tradition as decorating fir trees, feasting on goose, and the singing of carols. During the Victorian era many magazines printed ghost stories specifically for the Christmas season. These "winter tales" didn't necessarily explore Christmas themes. Rather, they were offered as an eerie pleasure to be enjoyed on Christmas Eve with the family, adding a supernatural shiver to the seasonal chill.

The tradition remained strong in the British Isles (and her colonies) throughout much of the twentieth century, though in recent years it has been on the wane. Certainly, few people in Canada or the United States seem to know about it any longer. This series of small books seeks to rectify this, to revive a charming custom for the long, dark nights we all know so well here at Christmastime.

THE HAUNTED BOOKSHELF

Charles Dickens
The Signalman

A.M. Burrage
One Who Saw

Edith Wharton
Afterward

M.R. James
The Diary of Mr. Poynter

Marjorie Bowen
The Crown Derby Plate

E.F. Benson
How Fear Departed the Long Gallery

W.W. Jacobs
The Toll House

Algernon Blackwood
The Empty House

H. Russell Wakefield
The Red Lodge

Walter de la Mare
The Green Room

THE HAUNTED BOOKSHELF

Frank Cowper
Christmas Eve on a Haunted Hulk

R.H. Malden
The Sundial

Elizabeth Gaskell
The Old Nurse's Story

Daphne du Maurier
The Apple Tree

Richard Bridgeman
The Morgan Trust

M.R. James
The Story of a Disappearance and an Appearance

Margaret Oliphant
The Open Door

Bernard Capes
An Eddy on the Floor

F. Marion Crawford
The Doll's Ghost

Edith Wharton
Mr. Jones

AN EDDY ON THE FLOOR

AN EDDY ON THE FLOOR

BERNARD CAPES

A GHOST STORY FOR CHRISTMAS

DESIGNED & DECORATED BY SETH

BIBLIOASIS

I had the pleasure of an invitation to one of those reunions or séances at the house, in a fashionable quarter, of my distant connection, Lady Barbara Grille, whereat it was my hostess's humour to gather together those many birds of alien feather and incongruous habit that will flock from the hedgerows to the least little flattering crumb of attention. And scarce one of them but thinks the simple feast is spread for him alone. And with so cheap a bait may a title lure.

That reference to so charming a personality should be in this place is a digression. She affects my narrative only inasmuch as I happened to meet at her house a gentleman who for a time exerted a considerable influence over my fortunes.

The next morning after the séance, my landlady entered with a card, which she presented to my consideration:

"Major James Shrike. H. M. Prison, D—"

All astonishment, I bade my visitor up.

He entered briskly, fur-collared, hat in hand, and bowed as he stood on the threshold. He was a very short man—snub-nosed; rusty-whiskered; indubitably and unimpressively a cockney in appearance. He might have walked out of a Cruikshank etching.

I was beginning, "May I enquire—" when the other took me up with a vehement frankness that I found engaging at once.

"This is a great intrusion. Will you pardon me? I heard some remarks of yours last night that deeply interested me. I obtained your name and address from our hostess, and took the liberty of—"

"Oh! Pray be seated. Say no more. My kinswoman's introduction is all-sufficient. I am happy in having caught your attention in so motley a crowd."

"She doesn't—forgive the impertinence—take herself seriously enough."

"Lady Barbara? Then you've found her out?"

"Ah!—you're not offended?"

"Not in the least."

"Good. It was a motley assemblage, as you say. Yet I'm inclined to think I found my pearl in the oyster. I'm afraid I interrupted—eh?"

"No, no, not at all. Only some idle scribbling. I'd finished."

"You are a poet?"

"Only a lunatic. I haven't taken my degree."

"Ah! It's a noble gift—the gift of song; precious through its rarity."

I caught a note of emotion in my visitor's voice, and glanced at him curiously.

"Surely," I thought, "that vulgar, ruddy little face is transfigured."

"But," said the stranger, coming to earth, "I am lingering beside the mark. I must try to justify my solecism in manners by a straight reference to the object of my visit. That is, in the first instance, a matter of business."

"Business!"

"I am a man with a purpose, seeking the hopefullest means to an end. Plainly: if I could procure you the post of resident doctor at D— gaol, would you be disposed to accept it?"

I looked my utter astonishment.

"I can affect no surprise at yours," said the visitor. "It is perfectly natural. Let me forestall some unnecessary expression of it. My offer seems unaccountable to you, seeing that we never met until last night. But I don't move entirely in the dark. I have ventured in the interval to inform myself as to the details of your career. I was entirely one with much of your expression of opinion as to the treatment of criminals, in which you controverted the crude and unpleasant scepticism of the lady you talked with. Combining the two, I come to the immediate conclusion that you are the man for my purpose."

"You have dumbfounded me. I don't know what to answer. You have views,

I know, as to prison treatment. Will you sketch them? Will you talk on, while I try to bring my scattered wits to a focus?"

"Certainly I will. Let me, in the first instance, recall to you a few words of your own. They ran somewhat in this fashion: is not the man of praetical genius the man who is most apt at solving the little problems of resourcefulness in life? Do you remember them?"

"Perhaps I do, in a cruder form."

"They attracted me at once. It is upon such a postulate I base my practice. Their moral is this:

"To know the antidote the moment the snake bites. That is to have the intuition of divinity. We shall rise to it some day, no doubt, and climb the hither side of the new Olympus. Who knows?

"Over the crest the spirit of creation may be ours."

I nodded, still at sea, and the other went on with a smile:

"I once knew a world-famous engineer with whom I used to breakfast occasionally. He had a patent egg-boiler on the table, with a little double-sided ladle underneath to hold the spirit. He complained that his egg was always undercooked. I said, 'Why not reverse the ladle so as to bring the deeper cut uppermost?' He was charmed with my perspicacity. The solution had never occurred to him. You remember, too, no doubt, the story of Coleridge and the horse collar. We aim too much at great developments. If we cultivate resourcefulness, the rest will follow. Shall I state my system in nuce? It is to encourage this spirit of resourcefulness."

"Surely the habitual criminal has it in a marked degree?"

"Yes; but abnormally developed in a single direction. His one object is to out-manoeuvre in a game of desperate and immoral chances. The tactical spirit in him has none of the higher ambition. It has felt itself in the degree only that stops at defiance."

"That is perfectly true."

"It is half self-conscious of an individuality that instinctively assumes the hopelessness of a recognition by duller intellects. Leaning to resentment through misguided vanity, it falls 'all oblique'. What is the cure for this? I answer, the teaching of a divine egotism. The subject must be led to a pure devotion to self. What he wishes to respect he must be taught to make beautiful and interesting. The policy of sacrifice to others has so long stunted his moral nature because it is a hypocritical policy. We are responsible to ourselves in the first instance; and to argue an eternal system of blind self-sacrifice is to undervalue the fine gift of individuality. In such he sees but an indefensible policy of force applied to the advantage of the community. He is told to be good—not that he may morally profit, but that others may not suffer inconvenience."

I was beginning to grasp, through my confusion, a certain clue of meaning in my visitor's rapid utterance. The stranger spoke fluently, but in the dry, positive voice that characterizes men of will.

"Pray go on," I said; "I am digesting in silence."

"We must endeavour to lead him to respect of self by showing him what his mind is capable of.

"I argue on no sectarian, no religious grounds even. Is it possible to make a man's self his most precious possession? Anyhow, I work to that end. A doctor purges before building up with a tonic. I eliminate cant and hypocrisy, and then introduce self-respect. It isn't enough to employ a man's hands only. Initiation in some labour that should prove wholesome and remunerative is a redeeming factor, but it isn't all. His mind must work also, and awaken to its capacities. If it rusts, the body reverts to inhuman instincts."

"May I ask how you—?"

"By intercourse—in my own person or through my officials. I wish to have only those about me who are willing to contribute to my designs, and with whom I can work in absolute harmony.

"All my officers are chosen to that end. No doubt a dash of constitutional sentimentalism gives colour to my theories. I get it from a human trait in me that circumstances have obliged me to put a hoarding round."

"I begin to gather daylight."

"Quite so. My patients are invited to exchange views with their guardians in a spirit of perfect friendliness; to solve little problems of practical moment; to acquire the pride of self-reliance.

"We have competitions, such as certain newspapers open to their readers in a simple form. I draw up the questions myself. The answers give me insight into the mental conditions of the competitors. Upon insight I proceed. I am fortunate in private means, and I am in a position to offer modest prizes to the winners. Whenever such a one is discharged, he finds awaiting him the tools most handy to his vocation. I bid him go forth in no pharisaical spirit, and invite him to communicate with me. I wish the shadow of the gaol to extend no further than the road whereon it lies. Henceforth, we are acquaintances with a common interest at heart. Isn't it monstrous that a state-fixed degree of misconduct should earn a man social ostracism? Parents are generally inclined to rule extra tenderness towards a child whose peccadilloes have brought him a whipping. For myself have no faith in police supervision. Give a culprit his term and have done with it. I find the majority who come back to me are ticket-of-leave men.

"Have I said enough? I offer you the reversion of the post. The present holder of it leaves in a month's time. Please to determine here and at once."

"Very good. I have decided."

"You will accept?"

"Yes."

WITH MY UNEXPECTED appointment as doctor to D— gaol, I seemed to have put on the seven-league boots of success. No doubt it was an extraordinary degree of good fortune, even to one who had looked forward with a broad view of confidence;

yet, I think, perhaps on account of the very casual nature of my promotion, I never took the post entirely seriously.

At the same time I was fully bent on justifying my little cockney patron's choice by a resolute subscription to his theories of prison management.

Major James Shrike inspired me with a curious conceit of impertinent respect. In person the very embodiment of that insignificant vulgarity, without extenuating circumstances, which is the type in caricature of the ultimate cockney, he possessed a force of mind and an earnestness of purpose that absolutely redeemed him on close acquaintanceship. I found him all he had stated himself to be, and something more.

He had a noble object always in view—the employment of sane and humanitarian methods in the treatment of redeemable criminals, and he strove towards it with

completely untiring devotion. He was of those who never insist beyond the limits of their own understanding, clear-sighted in discipline, frank in relaxation, an altruist in the larger sense.

His undaunted persistence, as I learned, received ample illustration some few years prior to my acquaintance with him, when—his system being experimental rather than mature—a devastating epidemic of typhoid in the prison had for the time stultified his efforts. He stuck to his post; but so virulent was the outbreak that the prison commissioners judged a complete evacuation of the building and overhauling of the drainage to be necessary. As a consequence, for some eighteen months—during thirteen of which the Governor and his household remained sole inmates of the solitary pile (so sluggishly do we redeem our condemned social bog-lands)—the "system" stood still for lack of material to mould. At the end of over a year of stagnation, a contract was accepted and workmen put in, and another five months saw the prison reordered for practical purposes.

The interval of forced inactivity must have sorely tried the patience of the Governor. Practical theorists condemned to rust too often eat out their own hearts. Major Shrike never referred to this period, and, indeed, laboriously snubbed any allusion to it.

He was, I have a shrewd notion, something of an officially petted reformer. Anyhow, to his abolition of the insensate barbarism of crank and treadmill in favour of civilizing methods no opposition was offered. Solitary confinement—a punishment outside all nature to a gregarious race—found no advocate in him. "A man's own suffering mind," he argued, "must be, of all moral food, the most poisonous for him to feed on. Surround a scorpion with fire and he stings himself to death, they say. Throw a diseased soul entirely upon its own resources and moral suicide results."

To sum up: his nature embodied humanity without sentimentalism, firmness without obstinacy, individuality without selfishness; his activity was boundless, his devotion to his system so real as to admit no utilitarian sophistries into his scheme of personal benevolence. Before I had been with him a week, I respected him as I had never respected man before.

ONE EVENING (it was during the second month of my appointment) we were sitting in his private study—a dark, comfortable room lined with books. It was an occasion on which a new characteristic of the man was offered to my inspection.

A prisoner of a somewhat unusual type had come in that day—a spiritualistic medium, convicted of imposture. To this person I casually referred.

"May I ask how you propose dealing with the newcomer?"

"On the familiar lines."

"But, surely—here we have a man of superior education, of imagination even?"

"No, no, no! A hawker's opportuneness; that describes it. These fellows would make death itself a vulgarity."

"You've no faith in their—"

"Not a tittle. Heaven forfend! A sheet and a turnip are poetry to their manifestations. It's as crude and sour soil for us to work on as any I know. We'll cart it wholesale."

"I take you—excuse my saying so—for a supremely sceptical man."

"As to what?"

"The supernatural."

There was no answer during a considerable interval. Presently it came, with deliberate insistence:

"It is a principle with me to oppose bullying. We are here for a definite purpose—his duty plain to any man who wills to read it. There may be disembodied spirits who seek to distress or annoy where they can no longer control. If there are, mine, which is not yet divorced from its means to material action, declines to be influenced by any irresponsible whimsy, emanating from a place whose denizens appear to be actuated by a mere frivolous antagonism to all human order and progress."

"But supposing you, a murderer, to be haunted by the presentment of your victim?"

"I will imagine that to be my case. Well, it makes no difference. My interest is with the great human system, in one of whose veins I am a circulating drop. It is my business to help to keep the system sound, to do my duty without fear or favour. If disease—say a fouled conscience—contaminates me, it is for me to throw off the incubus, not accept it, and transmit the poison.

"Whatever my lapses of nature, I owe it to the entire system to work for purity in my allotted sphere, and not to allow any microbe bugbear to ride me roughshod, to the detriment of my fellow drops."

I laughed.

"It should be for you," I said, "to learn to shiver, like the boy in the fairy-tale."

"I cannot," he answered, with a peculiar quiet smile; "and yet prisons, above all places, should be haunted."

VERY SHORTLY AFTER his arrival I was called to the cell of the medium, F—. He suffered, by his own statement, from severe pains in the head.

I found the man to be nervous, anaemic; his manner characterized by a sort of hysterical effrontery.

"Send me to the infirmary," he begged. "This isn't punishment, but torture."

"What are your symptoms?"

"I see things; my case has no comparison with others. To a man of my super-sensitiveness close confinement is mere cruelty."

I made a short examination. He was restless under my hands.

"You'll stay where you are," I said.

He broke out into violent abuse, and I left him.

Later in the day I visited him again. He was then white and sullen; but under his mood I could read real excitement of some sort.

"Now, confess to me, my man," I said, "what do you see?"

He eyed me narrowly, with his lips a little shaky.

"Will you have me moved if I tell you?"

"I can give no promise till I know."

He made up his mind after an interval of silence.

"There's something uncanny in my neighbourhood. Who's confined in the next cell—there, to the left?"

"To my knowledge it's empty."

He shook his head incredulously.

"Very well," I said, "I don't mean to bandy words with you;" and I turned to go.

At that he came after me with a frightened choke.

"Doctor, your mission's a merciful one. I'm not trying to sauce you. For God's sake have me moved! I can see further than most, I tell you!"

The fellow's manner gave me pause.

He was patently and beyond the pride of concealment terrified.

"What do you see?" I repeated stubbornly.

"It isn't that I see, but I know. The cell's not empty!" I stared at him in considerable wonderment.

"I will make enquiries," I said. "You may take that for a promise. If the cell proves empty, you stop where you are."

I noticed that he dropped his hands with a lost gesture as I left him. I was sufficiently moved to accost the warder who awaited me on the spot.

"Johnson," I said, "is that cell—"

"Empty, sir," answered the man sharply and at once.

Before I could respond, F— came suddenly to the door, which I still held open.

"You lying cur!" he shouted. "You damned lying cur!" The warder thrust the man back with violence.

"Now you, 49," he said, "dry up, and none of your sauce!" And he banged to the door with a sounding slap, and turned to me with a lowering face. The prisoner inside yelped and stormed at the studded panels.

"That cell's empty, sir," repeated Johnson.

"Will you, as a matter of conscience, let me convince myself? I promised the man."

"No, I can't."

"You can't?"

"No, sir."

"This is a piece of stupid discourtesy. You can have no reason, of course?"

"I can't open it—that's all."

"Oh, Johnson! Then I must go to the fountainhead."

"Very well, sir."

Quite baffled by the man's obstinacy, I said no more, but walked off. If my anger was roused, my curiosity was piqued in proportion.

I HAD NO opportunity of interviewing the Governor all day, but at night I visited him by invitation to play a game of piquet.

He was a man without "incumbrances"—as a severe conservatism designates the lares of the cottage—and, at home, lived at his ease and indulged his amusements without comment.

I found him "tasting" his books, with which the room was well lined, and drawing with relish at an excellent cigar in the intervals of the courses.

He nodded to me, and held out an open volume in his left hand. "Listen to this fellow," he said, tapping the page with his fingers:

"'The most tolerable sort of revenge is for those wrongs which there is no law to remedy; but then let a man take heed the revenge be such as there is no law to punish; else a man's enemy is still before-hand, and it is two for one. Some, when they take revenge, are desirous the party should know whence it cometh. This is the more generous. For the delight seemeth to be not so much in doing the hurt as in making the party repent. But base and crafty cowards are like the arrow that flieth in the dark. Cosmus, Duke of Florence, had a desperate saying against perfidious or neglecting friends, as if those wrongs were unpardonable: You shall read (saith he) that we are commanded to forgive our enemies; but you never read that we are commanded to forgive our friends.'"

"Is he not a rare fellow?"

"Who?" said I.

"Francis Bacon, who screwed his wit to his philosophy, like a hammer-head to its handle, and knocked a nail in at every blow. How many of our friends round about here would be picking oakum now if they had made a gospel of that quotation?"

"You mean they take no heed that the law may punish for that for which it gives no remedy?"

"Precisely; and specifically as to revenge. The criminal, from the murderer to the petty pilferer, is actuated solely by the spirit of vengeance—vengeance blind and speechless—towards a system that forces him into a position quite outside his natural instincts."

"As to that, we have left nature in the thicket. It is hopeless hunting for her now."

"We hear her breathing sometimes, my friend. Otherwise Her Majesty's prison locks would rust. But, I grant you, we have grown so unfamiliar with her that we call her simplest manifestations supernatural nowadays."

"That reminds me. I visited F— this afternoon. The man was in a queer way—not foxing, in my opinion. Hysteria, probably."

"Oh! What was the matter with him?"

"The form it took was some absurd prejudice about the next cell—number 47. He swore it was not empty—was quite upset about it—said there was some infernal influence at work in his neighbourhood. Nerves, he finds, I suppose, may revenge themselves on one who has made a habit of playing tricks with them. To satisfy him, I asked Johnson to open the door of the next cell—"

"He refused."

"It is closed by my orders."

"That settles it, of course. The manner of Johnson's refusal was a bit uncivil, but—"

He had been looking at me intently all this time—so intently that I was conscious of a little embarrassment and confusion. His mouth was set like a dash between brackets, and his eyes glistened. Now his features relaxed, and he gave a short high neigh of a laugh.

"My dear fellow, you must make allowances for the rough old lurcher. He was a soldier. He is all cut and measured out to the regimental pattern. With him Major Shrike, like the king, can do no wrong. Did I ever tell you he served under me in India? He did; and, moreover, I saved his life there."

"In an engagement?"

"Worse—from the bite of a snake. It was a mere question of will. I told him to wake and walk, and he did. They had thought him already in rigor mortis; and, as for him—well, his devotion to me since has been single to the last degree."

"That's as it should be."

"To be sure. And he's quite in my confidence. You must pass over the old beggar's churlishness."

I laughed an assent. And then an odd thing happened. As I spoke, I had walked over to a bookcase on the opposite side of the room to that on which my host stood. Near this bookcase hung a mirror—an oblong affair, set in brass repoussé work—on the wall; and, happening to glance into it as I approached, I caught sight of the Major's reflection as he turned his face to follow my movement.

I say "turned his face"—a formal description only. What met my startled gaze was an image of some nameless horror—of features grooved, and battered, and shapeless, as if they had been torn by a wild beast.

I gave a little indrawn gasp and turned about. There stood the Major, plainly himself, with a pleasant smile on his face.

"What's up?" said he.

He spoke abstractedly, pulling at his cigar; and I answered rudely, "That's a damned bad looking-glass of yours!"

"I didn't know there was anything wrong with it," he said, still abstracted and apart. And, indeed, when by sheer mental effort I forced myself to look again, there stood my companion as he stood in the room.

I gave a tremulous laugh, muttered something or nothing, and fell to examining the books in the case. But my fingers shook a trifle as I aimlessly pulled out one volume after another.

"Am I getting fanciful?" I thought—"I whose business it is to give practical account of every bugbear of the nerves.

Bah! My liver must be out of order. A speck of bile in one's eye may look a flying dragon."

I dismissed the folly from my mind, and set myself resolutely to inspecting the books marshalled before me. Roving amongst them, I pulled out, entirely at random, a thin, worn duodecimo, that was thrust well back at a shelf end, as if it shrank from comparison with its prosperous and portly neighbours. Nothing but chance impelled me to the choice; and I don't know to this day what the ragged volume was about. It opened naturally at a marker that lay in it—a folded slip of paper, yellow with age; and glancing at this, a printed name caught my eye.

With some stir of curiosity, I spread the slip out. It was a title-page to a volume, of poems, presumably; and the author was James Shrike.

I uttered an exclamation, and turned, book in hand.

"An author!" I said. "You an author, Major Shrike!"

To my surprise, he snapped round upon me with something like a glare of fury on his face.

This the more startled me as I believed I had reason to regard him as a man whose principles of conduct had long disciplined a temper that was naturally hasty enough.

Before I could speak to explain, he had come hurriedly across the room and had rudely snatched the paper out of my hand.

"How did this get—" he began; then in a moment came to himself, and apologized for his ill manners.

"I thought every scrap of the stuff had been destroyed," he said, and tore the page into fragments. "It is an ancient effusion, doctor—perhaps the greatest folly of my life; but it's something of a sore subject with me, and I shall be obliged if you'll not refer to it again."

He courted my forgiveness so frankly that the matter passed without embarrassment; and we had our game and spent a genial evening together. But memory of the queer little scene stuck in my mind, and I could not forbear pondering it fitfully.

Surely here was a new side-light that played upon my friend and superior a little fantastically.

CONSCIOUS OF A certain vague wonder in my mind, I was traversing the prison, lost in thought, after my sociable evening with the Governor, when the fact that dim light was issuing from the open door of cell number 49 brought me to myself and to a pause in the corridor outside.

Then I saw that something was wrong

with the cell's inmate, and that my services were required.

The medium was struggling on the floor, in what looked like an epileptic fit, and Johnson and another warder were holding him from doing an injury to himself.

The younger man welcomed my appearance with relief.

"Heard him guggling," he said, "and thought as something were up. You come timely, sir."

More assistance was procured, and I ordered the prisoner's removal to the infirmary. For a minute, before following him, I was left alone with Johnson.

"It came to a climax, then?" I said, looking the man steadily in the face.

"He may be subject to 'em, sir," he replied evasively.

I walked deliberately up to the closed door of the adjoining cell, which was the last on that side of the corridor. Huddled against the massive end wall, and half embedded in it, as it seemed, it lay in a certain shadow, and bore every sign of dust and disuse. Looking closely, I saw that the trap in the door was not only firmly bolted, but screwed into its socket.

I turned and said to the warder quietly—"Is it long since this cell was in use?"

"You're very fond of asking questions," he answered doggedly.

It was evident he would baffle me by impertinence rather than yield a confidence. A queer insistence had seized me—a strange desire to know more about this mysterious chamber. But, for all my curiosity, I flushed at the man's tone.

"You have your orders," I said sternly, "and do well to hold by them. I doubt, nevertheless, if they include impertinence to your superiors."

"I look straight on my duty, sir," he said, a little abashed. "I don't wish to give offence."

He did not, I feel sure. He followed his instinct to throw me off the scent, that was all.

I strode off in a fume, and after attending F— in the infirmary, went promptly to my own quarters.

I was in an odd frame of mind, and for long tramped my sitting-room to and fro, too restless to go to bed, or, as an alternative, to settle down to a book. There was a welling up in my heart of some emotion that I could neither trace nor define. It seemed neighbour to terror, neighbour to an intense fainting pity, yet was not distinctly either of these. Indeed, where was cause for one, or the subject of the other? F— might have endured mental sufferings which it was only human to help to end, yet F— was a swindling rogue, who, once relieved, merited no further consideration.

It was not on him my sentiments were wasted. Who, then, was responsible for them?

There was a very plain line of demarcation between the legitimate spirit of enquiry and mere apish curiosity. I could recognize it, I have no doubt, as a rule, yet in my then mood, under the influence of a kind of morbid seizure, inquisitiveness took me by the throat. I could not whistle my mind from the chase of a certain graveyard will-o'-wisp; and on it went stumbling and floundering through bog and mire, until it fell into a state of collapse, and was useful for nothing else.

I went to bed and to sleep without difficulty, but I was conscious of myself all the time, and of a shadowless horror that seemed to come stealthily out of corners and to bend over and look at me, and to be nothing but a curtain or a hanging coat when I started and stared.

Over and over again this happened, and my temperature rose by leaps, and suddenly I saw that if I failed to assert myself, and promptly, fever would lap me in a consuming fire. Then in a moment I broke into a profuse perspiration, and sank exhausted into delicious unconsciousness.

Morning found me restored to vigour, but still with the maggot of curiosity in my brain. It worked there all day, and for many subsequent days, and at last it seemed as if my every faculty were honeycombed with its ramifications. Then "this will not do," I thought, but still the tunnelling process went on.

At first I would not acknowledge to myself what all this mental to-do was about. I was ashamed of my new development, in fact, and nervous, too, in a degree of what it might reveal in the matter of moral degeneration; but gradually, as the curious devil mastered me, I grew into such harmony with it that I could shut my eyes no longer to the true purpose of its insistence. It was the closed cell about which my thoughts hovered like crows circling round carrion.

"IN THE DEAD waste and middle" of a certain night I awoke with a strange, quick recovery of consciousness. There was the passing of a single expiration, and I had been asleep and was awake. I had gone to bed with no sense of premonition or of resolve in a particular direction; I sat up a monomaniac. It was as if, swelling in the silent hours, the tumour of curiosity had come to a head, and in a moment it was necessary to operate upon it.

I make no excuse for my then condition. I am convinced I was the victim of some undistinguishable force, that I was an agent under the control of the supernatural, if you like.

Some thought had been in my mind of late that in my position it was my duty to unriddle the mystery of the closed cell. This was a sop timidly held out to and rejected by my better reason. I sought—and I knew it in my heart—solution of the puzzle, because it was a puzzle with an atmosphere that vitiated my moral fibre. Now, suddenly, I knew I must act, or, by forcing self-control, imperil my mind's stability.

All strung to a sort of exaltation, I rose noiselessly and dressed myself with rapid, nervous hands. My every faculty was focused upon a solitary point. Without and around there was nothing but shadow and uncertainty. I seemed conscious only of a shaft of light, as it were, traversing the darkness and globing itself in a steady disc of radiance on a lonely door.

Slipping out into the great echoing vault of the prison in stockinged feet, I sped with no hesitation of purpose in the direction of the corridor that was my goal. Surely some resolute Providence guided and encompassed me, for no meeting with the night patrol occurred at any point to embarrass or deter me. Like a ghost myself, I flitted along the stone flags of the passages, hardly waking a murmur from them in my progress.

Without, I knew, a wild and stormy wind thundered on the walls of the prison. Within, where the very atmosphere was self-contained, a cold and solemn peace held like an irrevocable judgement.

I found myself as if in a dream before the sealed door that had for days harassed

my waking thoughts. Dim light from a distant gas jet made a patch of yellow upon one of its panels; the rest was buttressed with shadow.

A sense of fear and constriction was upon me as I drew softly from my pocket a screwdriver I had brought with me. It never occurred to me, I swear, that the quest was no business of mine, and that even now I could withdraw from it, and no one be the wiser. But I was afraid—I was afraid. And there was not even the negative comfort of knowing that the neighbouring cell was tenanted. It gaped like a ghostly garret next door to a deserted house.

What reason had I to be there at all, or, being there, to fear? I can no more explain than tell how it was that I, an impartial follower of my vocation, had allowed myself to be tricked by that in the nerves I had made it my interest to study and combat in others.

My hand that held the tool was cold and wet. The stiff little shriek of the first screw, as it turned at first uneasily in its socket, sent a jarring thrill through me. But I persevered, and it came out readily by-and-by, as did the four or five others that held the trap secure.

Then I paused a moment; and, I confess, the quick pant of fear seemed to come grey from my lips. There were sounds about me—the deep breathing of imprisoned men; and I envied the sleepers their hard-wrung repose.

At last, in one access of determination, I put out my hand and sliding back the bolt, hurriedly flung open the trap. An acrid whiff of dust assailed my nostrils as I stepped back a pace and stood expectant of anything—or nothing. What did I wish, or dread, or foresee? The complete absurdity of my behaviour was revealed to me in a moment. I could shake off the incubus here and now, and be a sane man again.

I giggled, with an actual ring of self-contempt in my voice, as I made a forward movement to close the aperture. I advanced my face to it, and inhaled the sluggish air that stole forth, and—God in heaven!

I had staggered back with that cry in my throat, when I felt fingers like iron clamps close on my arm and hold it. The grip, more than the face I turned to look upon in my surging terror, was forcibly human.

It was the warder Johnson who had seized me, and my heart bounded as I met the cold fury of his eyes.

"Prying!" he said, in a hoarse, savage whisper. "So you will, will you? And now let the devil help you!"

It was not this fellow I feared, though his white face was set like a demon's; and in the thick of my terror I made a feeble attempt to assert my authority.

"Let me go!" I muttered. "What! You dare?"

In his frenzy he shook my arm as a terrier shakes a rat, and, like a dog, he held on, daring me to release myself.

For the moment an instinct half-murderous leapt in me. It sank and was overwhelmed in a slough of some more secret emotion.

"Oh!" I whispered, collapsing, as it were, to the man's fury, even pitifully deprecating it. "What is it? What's there? It drew me—something unnameable."

He gave a snapping laugh like a cough. His rage waxed second by second. There was a maniacal suggestiveness in it; and not much longer, it was evident, could he have it under control. I saw it run and congest in his eyes; and, on the instant of its accumulation, he tore at me with a sudden wild strength, and drove me up against the very door of the secret cell.

The action, the necessity of self-defence, restored me to some measure of dignity and sanity.

"Let me go, you ruffian!" I cried, struggling to free myself from his grasp.

It was useless. He held me madly. There was no beating him off: and, so holding me, he managed to produce a single key from one of his pockets, and to slip it with a rusty clang into the lock of the door.

"You dirty, prying civilian!" he panted at me, as he swayed this way and that with the pull of my body. "You shall have your wish, by G—! You want to see inside, do you? Look, then!"

He dashed open the door as he spoke, and pulled me violently into the opening. A great waft of the cold, dank air came at us, and with it—what?

The warder had jerked his dark lantern from his belt, and now—an arm of his still clasped about one of mine—snapped the slide open.

"Where is it?" he muttered, directing the disc of light round and about the floor of the cell. I ceased struggling. Some counter influence was raising an odd curiosity in me.

"Ah!" he cried, in a stifled voice, "there you are, my friend!" He was setting the light slowly travelling along the stone flags close by the wall over against us, and now, so guiding it, looked askance at me with a small, greedy smile.

"Follow the light, sir," he whispered jeeringly.

I looked, and saw twirling on the floor, in the patch of radiance cast by the lamp, a little eddy of dust, it seemed. This eddy was never still, but went circling in that stagnant place without apparent cause or influence; and, as it circled, it moved slowly on by wall and corner, so that presently in its progress it must reach us where we stood.

Now, draughts will play queer freaks in quiet places, and of this trifling phenomenon I should have taken little note ordinarily. But, I must say at once, that as I gazed upon the odd moving thing my heart seemed to fall in upon itself like a drained artery.

"Johnson!" I cried, "I must get out of this. I don't know what's the matter, or—why do you hold me? D—it! Man, let me go; let me go, I say!"

As I grappled with him he dropped the lantern with a crash and flung his arms violently about me.

"You don't!" he panted, the muscles of his bent and rigid neck seeming actually to cut into my shoulder-blade. "You don't, by G—! You came of your own accord, and now you shall take your bellyfull!"

It was a struggle for life or death, or, worse, for life and reason. But I was young and wiry, and held my own, if I could do little more. Yet there was something to combat beyond the mere brute strength of the man I struggled with, for I fought in an atmosphere of horror unexplainable, and I knew that inch by inch the thing on the floor was circling round in our direction.

Suddenly in the breathing darkness I felt it close upon us, gave one mortal yell of fear, and, with a last despairing fury, tore myself from the encircling arms, and sprang into the corridor without. As I plunged and leapt, the warder clutched at me, missed, caught a foot on the edge of the door, and, as the latter whirled to with a clap, fell heavily at my feet in a fit. Then, as I stood staring down upon him, steps sounded along the corridor and the voices of scared men hurrying up.

ILL AND SHAKEN, and, for the time, little in love with life, yet fearing death as I had never dreaded it before, I spent the rest of that horrible night huddled between my crumpled sheets, fearing to look forth, fearing to think, wild only to be far away, to be housed in some green and innocent hamlet, where I might forget the madness and the terror in learning to walk the unvext paths of placid souls. That unction I could lay to my heart, at least. I had done the manly part by the stricken warder, whom I had attended to his own home, in a row of little tenements that stood south of the prison walls. I had replied to all enquiries with some dignity and spirit, attributing my ruffled condition to an assault on the part of Johnson, when he was already under the shadow of his seizure. I had directed his removal, and grudged him no professional attention that it was in my power to bestow. But afterwards, locked into my room, my whole nervous system broke up like a trodden ant-hill, leaving me conscious of nothing but an aimless scurrying terror and the black swarm of thoughts, so that I verily fancied my reason would give under the strain.

Yet I had more to endure and to triumph over.

Near morning I fell into a troubled sleep, throughout which the drawn twitch of muscle seemed an accent on every word of ill-omen I had ever spelt out of the alphabet of fear. If my body rested, my brain was an open chamber for any toad of ugliness that listed to "sit at squat" in.

Suddenly I woke to the fact that there was a knocking at my door—that there had been for some little time.

I cried, "Come in!" finding a weak restorative in the mere sound of my own human voice; then, remembering the key was turned, bade the visitor wait until I could come to him.

Scrambling, feeling dazed and white-livered, out of bed, I opened the door, and met one of the warders on the threshold. The man looked scared, and his lips, I noticed, were set in a somewhat boding fashion.

"Can you come at once, sir?" he said. "There's summat wrong with the Governor."

"Wrong? What's the matter with him?"

"Why,"—he looked down, rubbed an imaginary protuberance smooth with his foot, and glanced up at me again with a quick, furtive expression—"he's got his face set in the grating of 47, and danged if a man Jack of us can get him to move or speak."

I turned away, feeling sick. I hurriedly pulled on coat and trousers, and hurriedly went off with my summoner. Reason was all absorbed in a wildest phantasy of apprehension.

"Who found him?" I muttered, as we sped on.

"Vokins see him go down the corridor about half after eight, sir, and see him give a start like when he noticed the trap open. It's never been so before in my time. Johnson must ha' done it last night, before he were took."

"Yes, yes."

"The man said the Governor went to shut it, it seemed, and to draw his face to'ards the bars in so doin'. Then he see him a-lookin' through, as he thought; but nat'rally it weren't no business of his'n, and he went off about his work. But when he come anigh agen, fifteen minutes later, there were the Governor in the same position; and he got scared over it, and called out to one or two of us."

"Why didn't one of you ask the Major if anything was wrong?"

"Bless you! We did; and no answer. And we pulled him, compatible with discipline, but—"

"But what?"

"He's stuck."

"Stuck!"

"See for yourself, sir. That's all I ask."

I did, a moment later. A little group was collected about the door of cell 47, and the members of it spoke together in whispers, as if they were frightened men. One young fellow, with a face white in patches, as if it had been floured, slid from them as I approached, and accosted me tremulously.

"Don't go anigh, sir. There's something wrong about the place."

I pulled myself together, forcibly beating down the excitement reawakened by the associations of the spot. In the discomfiture of others' nerves I found my own restoration.

"Don't be an ass!" I said, in a determined voice. "There's nothing here that can't be explained. Make way for me, please!"

They parted and let me through, and I saw him. He stood, spruce, frock-coated, dapper, as he always was, with his face pressed against and into the grill, and either hand raised and clenched tightly round a bar of the trap. His posture was as of one caught and striving frantically to release himself; yet the narrowness of the interval between the rails precluded so extravagant an idea. He stood quite motionless—taut and on the strain, as it were—and nothing of his face was visible but the back ridges of his jawbones, showing white through a bush of red whiskers.

"Major Shrike!" I rapped out, and, allowing myself no hesitation, reached forth my hand and grasped his shoulder. The body vibrated under my touch, but he neither answered nor made sign of hearing me. Then I pulled at him forcibly, and ever with increasing strength. His fingers held like steel braces. He seemed glued to the trap, like Theseus to the rock.

Hastily I peered round, to see if I could get a glimpse of his face. I noticed enough to send me back with a little stagger.

"Has none of you got a key to this door?" I asked, reviewing the scared faces about me, than which my own was no less troubled, I feel sure.

"Only the Governor, sir," said the warder who had fetched me. "There's not a man but him amongst us that ever seen this opened."

He was wrong there, I could have told him; but held my tongue, for obvious reasons.

"I want it opened. Will one of you feel in his pockets?"

Not a soul stirred. Even had not sense of discipline precluded, that of a certain inhuman atmosphere made fearful creatures of them all.

"Then," said I, "I must do it myself."

I turned once more to the stiff-strung figure, had actually put hand on it, when an exclamation from Vokins arrested me.

"There's a key—there, sir!" he said— "stickin' out yonder between his feet."

Sure enough there was—Johnson's, no doubt, that had been shot from its socket by the clapping to of the door, and afterwards kicked aside by the warder in his convulsive struggles.

I stooped, only too thankful for the respite, and drew it forth. I had seen it but once before, yet I recognized it at a glance.

Now, I confess, my heart felt ill as I slipped the key into the wards, and a sickness of resentment at the tyranny of Fate in making me its helpless minister surged up in my veins.

Once, with my fingers on the iron loop, I paused, and ventured a fearful side glance at the figure whose crooked elbow almost touched my face; then, strung to the high pitch of inevitability, I shot the lock, pushed at the door, and in the act, made a back leap into the corridor.

Scarcely, in doing so, did I look for the totter and collapse outwards of the rigid form. I had expected to see it fall away, face down, into the cell, as its support swung from it. Yet it was, I swear, as if something from within had relaxed its grasp and given the fearful dead man a swingeing push outwards as the door opened.

It went on its back, with a dusty slap on the stone flags, and from all its spectators—me included—came a sudden drawn sound, like a wind in a keyhole.

What can I say, or how describe it? A dead thing it was—but the face!

Barred with livid scars where the grating rails had crossed it, the rest seemed to have been worked and kneaded into a mere featureless plate of yellow and expressionless flesh.

And it was this I had seen in the glass!

THERE WAS AN interval following the experience above narrated, during which a certain personality that had once been mine was effaced or suspended, and I seemed a passive creature, innocent of the least desire of independence. It was not that I was actually ill or actually insane.

A merciful Providence set my finer wits slumbering, that was all, leaving me a sufficiency of the grosser faculties that were necessary to the right ordering of my behaviour.

I kept to my room, it is true, and even lay a good deal in bed; but this was more to satisfy the busy scruples of a locum tenens—a practitioner of the neighbourhood, who came daily to the prison to officiate in my absence—than to cosset a complaint that in its inactivity was purely negative. I could review what had happened with a calmness as profound as if I had read of it in a book. I could have wished to continue my duties, indeed, had the power of insistence remained to me. But the saner medicus was acute where I had gone blunt, and bade me to the restful course. He was right. I was mentally stunned, and had I not slept off my lethargy, I should have gone mad in an hour—leapt at a bound, probably, from inertia to flaming lunacy.

I remembered everything, but through a fluffy atmosphere, so to speak. It was as if I looked on bygone pictures through ground glass that softened the ugly outlines.

Sometimes I referred to these to my substitute, who was wise to answer me according to my mood; for the truth left me unruffled, whereas an obvious evasion of it would have distressed me.

"Hammond," I said one day, "I have never yet asked you. How did I give my evidence at the inquest?"

"Like a doctor and a sane man."

"That's good. But it was a difficult course to steer. You conducted the post-mortem. Did any peculiarity in the dead man's face strike you?"

"Nothing but this: that the excessive contraction of the bicipital muscles had brought the features into such forcible contact with the bars as to cause bruising and actual abrasion. He must have been dead some little time when you found him."

"And nothing else? You noticed nothing else in his face—a sort of obliteration of what makes one human, I mean?"

"Oh, dear, no! Nothing but the painful constriction that marks any ordinary fatal attack of angina pectoris.—There's a rum breach of promise case in the paper today. You should read it; it'll make you laugh."

I had no more inclination to laugh than to sigh; but I accepted the change of subject with an equanimity now habitual to me.

ONE MORNING I sat up in bed, and knew that consciousness was wide awake in me once more. It had slept, and now rose refreshed, but trembling. Looking back, all in a flutter of new responsibility, along the misty path by way of which I had recently loitered, I shook with an awful thankfulness at sight of the pitfalls I had skirted and escaped—of the demons my witlessness had baffled.

The joy of life was in my heart again, but chastened and made pitiful by experience.

Hammond noticed the change in me directly he entered, and congratulated me upon it.

"Go slow at first, old man," he said. "You've fairly sloughed the old skin; but give the sun time to toughen the new one. Walk in it at present, and be content."

I was, in great measure, and I followed his advice. I got leave of absence, and ran down for a month in the country to a certain house we wot of, where kindly ministration to my convalescence was only one of the many blisses to be put to an account of rosy days.

"Then did my love awake,
Most like a lily-flower,
And as the lovely queene of heaven,
So shone shee in her bower."

Ah, me! Ah, me! When was it? A year ago, or two-thirds of a lifetime? Alas! "Age with stealing steps hath clawde me with his erowch." And will the yews root in my heart, I wonder?

I was well, sane, recovered, when one morning, towards the end of my visit, I received a letter from Hammond, enclosing a packet addressed to me, and jealously sealed and fastened. My friend's communication ran as follows:

There died here yesterday afternoon a warder, Johnson—he who had that apo-

plectic seizure, you will remember, the night before poor Shrike's exit. I attended him to the end, and, being alone with him an hour before the finish, he took the enclosed from under his pillow, and a solemn oath from me that I would forward it direct to you sealed as you will find it, and permit no other soul to examine or even touch it. I acquit myself of the charge, but, my dear fellow, with an uneasy sense of the responsibility I incur in thus possibly suggesting to you a retrospect of events which you had much best consign to the limbo of the—not inexplainable, but not worth trying to explain. It was patent from what I have gathered that you were in an overstrung and excitable condition at that time, and that your temporary collapse was purely nervous in its character. It seems there was some nonsense abroad in the prison about a certain cell, and that there were fools who thought fit to associ-

ate Johnson's attack and the other's death with the opening of that cell's door. I have given the new Governor a tip, and he has stopped all that. We have examined the cell in company, and found it, as one might suppose, a very ordinary chamber. The two men died perfectly natural deaths, and there is the last to be said on the subject. I mention it only from the fear that the enclosed may contain some allusion to the rubbish, a perusal of which might check the wholesome convalescence of your thoughts. If you take my advice, you will throw the packet into the fire unread. At least, if you do examine it, postpone the duty till you feel impervious to any mental trickery, and—bear in mind that you are a worthy member of a particularly matter-of-fact and unemotional profession.

I SMILED AT the last clause, for I was now

in a condition to feel a rather warm shame over my erst weak-knee'd collapse before a sheet and an illuminated turnip. I took the packet to my bedroom, shut the door, and sat myself down by the open window. The garden lay below me, and the dewy meadows beyond. In the one, bees were busy ruffling the ruddy gillyflowers and April stocks; in the other, the hedge twigs were all frosted with Mary buds, as if Spring had brushed them with the fleece of her wings in passing.

I fetched a sigh of content as I broke the seal of the packet and brought out the enclosure.

Somewhere in the garden a little sardonic laugh was clipt to silence. It came from groom or maid, no doubt; yet it thrilled me with an odd feeling of uncanniness, and I shivered slightly.

"Bah!" I said to myself determinedly.

"There is a shrewd nip in the wind, for all the show of sunlight;" and I rose, pulled down the window, and resumed my seat.

Then in the closed room, that had become deathly quiet by contrast, I opened and read the dead man's letter.

Sir, I hope you will read what I here put down. I lay it on you as a solemn injunction, for I am a dying man, and I know it. And to who is my death due, and the Governor's death, if not to you, for your pryin' and curiosity, as surely as if you had drove a nife through our harts? Therefore, I say, Read this, and take my burden from me, for it has been a burden; and now it is right that you that interfered should have it on your own mortal shoulders. The Major is dead and I am dying, and in the first of my fit it went on in my head like cimbells that the trap was left open, and that if he passed he would look in and it would get him. For he knew not fear, neither would he submit to bullying by God or devil.

Now I will tell you the truth, and Heaven quit you of your responsibility in our destruction.

There wasn't another man to me like the Governor in all the countries of the world. Once he brought me to life after doctors had given me up for dead; but he willed it, and I lived; and ever afterwards I loved him as a dog loves it master. That was in the Punjab; and I came home to England with him, and was his servant when he got his appointment to the jail here. I tell you he was a proud and fierce man, but under control and tender to those he favoured; and I will tell you also a strange thing about him. Though he was a soldier and an officer, and strict in discipline as made men fear and admire him, his hart at bottom was all for books, and literature, and such-like gentle crafts. I had his confidence, as a man gives his confidence to his dog, and before others. In this way I learnt the bitter sorrow of his life. He had once hoped to be a poet, acknowledged as such before the world. He was by natur' an idelist, as they call it, and God knows what it meant to him to come out of the woods, so to speak, and swet in the dust of cities; but he did it, for his will was of tempered steel. He buried his dreams in the clouds and came down to earth greatly resolved, but with one undying hate. It is not good to hate as he could, and worse to be hated by such as him; and I will tell you the story, and what it led to.

It was when he was a subaltern that he made up his mind to the plunge. For years he had placed all his hopes and confidents in a book of verses he had wrote, and added to, and improved during that time. A little *encouragement, a little word of praise, was all he looked for, and then he was redy to buckle to again, profitin' by advice, and do better. He put all the love and beauty of his hart into that book, and at last, after doubt, and anguish, and much diffidents, he published it, and give it to the world. Sir, it fell what they call still-born from the press. It was like a green leaf flutterin' down in a dead wood. To a proud and hopeful man, bubblin' with music, the pain of neglect, when he come to relize it, was terrible. But nothing was said, and there was nothing to say. In silence he had to endure and suffer.*

But one day, during manoovers, there came to the camp a grey-faced man, a newspaper correspondent, and young Shrike nocked up a friendship with him. Now how it come about I cannot tell, but so it did that this skip-kennel wormed the lad's sorrow out of him, and his confidents, swore he'd been damnabilly used, and that when he got back he'd crack up the book himself in his own paper. He was a fool for his pains, and a serpent in his croolty. The notice come out as promised, and, my God! The author was laughed and mocked at from beginning to end. Even confidentses he had given to the creature was twisted to his ridicule, and his very appearance joked over. And the mess got wind of it, and made a rare story for the dog days.

He bore it like a soldier and that he became hart and liver from the moment. But he put something to the account of the grey-faced man and locked it up in his breast.

He come across him again years after-wards in India, and told him very politely that he hadn't forgotten him, and didn't intend to. But he was anigh losin' sight of him there for ever and a day, for the creature took cholera, or what looked like it, and rubbed shoulders with death and the devil before he pulled through. And he come across him again over here, and that was the last of him, as you shall see presently.

Once, after I knew the Major (he were Captain then), I was a-brushin' his coat, and he stood a long while before the glass. Then he twisted upon me, with a smile on his mouth, and says he—"The dog was right, Johnson: this isn't the face of a poet. I was a presumtious ass, and born to cast up figgers with a pen behind my ear."

"Captain," I says, "if you was skinned, you'd look like any other man without his. The quality of a soul isn't expressed by a coat."

"Well," he answers, "my soul's pretty clean-swept, I think, save for one Bluebeard chamber in it that's been kep' locked ever so many years. It's nice and dirty by this time, I expect," he says. Then the grin comes on his mouth again. "I'll open it some day," he says, "and look. There's something in it about comparing me to a dancing dervish, with the wind in my petticuts. Perhaps I'll get the chance to set somebody else dancing by-and-by."

He did, and took it, and the Bluebeard chamber come to be opened in this very jail.

It was when the system was lying fallow, so to speak, and the prison was deserted. Nobody was there but him and me and the echoes from the empty courts. The contract for restoration hadn't been signed, and for months, and more than a year, we lay idle, nothing bein' done.

Near the beginnin' of this period, one day comes, for the third time of the Major's seein' him, the grey-faced man. "Let bygones be bygones," he says. "I was a good friend to you, though you didn't know it; and now, I expect, you're in the way to thank me."

"I am," says the Major.

"Of course," he answers. "Where would be your fame and reputation as one of the leadin' prison reformers of the day if you had kep' on in that timing nonsense?"

"Have you come for my thanks?" says the Governor.

"I've come," says the grey-faced man, "to examine and report upon your system."

"For your paper?"

"Possibly; but to satisfy myself of its efficacy, in the first instance."

"You aren't commissioned, then?"

"No; I come on my own responsibility."

"Without consultation with any one?"

"Absolutely without. I haven't even a wife to advise me," he says, with a yellow grin. What once passed for cholera had set the bile on his skin like paint, and he had caught a manner of coughing behind his hand like a toast-master.

"I know," says the Major, looking him

steady in the face, "that what you say about me and my affairs is sure to be actuated by conscientious motives."

"Ah," he answers. "You're sore about that review still, I see."

"Not at all," says the Major; "and, in proof, I invite you to be my guest for the night, and tomorrow I'll show you over the prison and explain my system."

The creature cried, "Done!" and they set to and discussed jail matters in great earnestness. I couldn't guess the Governor's intentions, but, somehow, his manner troubled me. And yet I can remember only one point of his talk. He were always dead against making public show of his birds. "They're there for reformation, not ignominy," he'd say. Prisons in the old days were often, with the asylum and the work'us, made the holiday showplaces of towns. I've heard of one Justice of the Peace, up North, who, to save himself trouble, used to sign a lot of blank orders for leave to view, so that applicants needn't bother him when they wanted to go over. They've changed all that, and the Governor were instrumental in the change.

"It's against my rule," he said that night, "to exhibit to a stranger without a Government permit; but, seein' the place is empty, and for old remembrance' sake, I'll make an exception in your favour, and you shall learn all I can show you of the inside of a prison."

Now this was natural enough; but I was uneasy.

He treated his guest royally; so much that when we assembled the next mornin' for the inspection, the grey-faced man were shaky as a wet dog. But the Major were all set prim and dry, like the soldier he was.

We went straight away down corridor B, and at cell 47 we stopped.

"We will begin our inspection here," said the Governor. "Johnson, open the door."

I had the keys of the row; fitted in the right one, and pushed open the door.

"After you, sir," said the Major; and the creature walked in, and he shut the door on him.

I think he smelt a rat at once, for he began beating on the wood and calling out to us. But the Major only turned round to me with his face like a stone.

"Take that key from the bunch," he said, "and give it to me."

I obeyed, all in a tremble, and he took and put it in his pocket.

"My God, Major," I whispered, "what are you going to do with him?"

"Silence, sir!" he said; "How dare you question your superior officer!"

And the noise inside grew louder.

The Governor, he listened to it a moment like music; then he unbolted and flung open the trap, and the creature's face came at it like a wild beast's.

"Sir," said the Major to it, "you can't better understand my system than by experiencing it. What an article for your paper you could write already—almost as pungint a one as that in which you ruined the hopes and prospects of a young cockney poet."

The man mouthed at the bars. He was half-mad, I think, in that one minute.

"Let me out!" he screamed. "This is a hidius joke! Let me out!"

"When you are quite quiet—deathly quiet," said the Major, "you shall come out. Not before;" and he shut the trap in its face very softly.

"Come, Johnson, march!" he said, and took the lead, and we walked out of the prison.

I was like to faint, but I dared not disobey, and the man's screeching followed us all down the empty corridors and halls, *until we shut the first great door on it.*

It may have gone on for hours, alone in that awful emptiness. The creature was a reptile, but the thought sickened my heart.

And from that hour till his death, five months later, he rotted and maddened in his dreadful tomb.

THERE WAS MORE, but I pushed the ghastly confession from me at this point in uncontrollable loathing and terror. Was it possible—possible, that injured vanity could so falsify its victim's every tradition of decency?

"Oh!" I muttered, "what a disease is ambition! Who takes one step towards it puts his foot on Alsirat!"

It was minutes before my shocked nerves were equal to a resumption of the task; but at last I took it up again, with a groan.

I don't think at first I realized the full mischief the Governor intended to do. At least, I hoped he only meant to give the man a good fright and then let him go. I might have known better. How could he ever release him without ruining himself?

The next morning he summoned me to attend him. There was a strange new look of triumph in his face, and in his hand he held a heavy hunting-crop. I pray to God he acted in madness, but my duty and obedience was to him.

"There is sport towards, Johnson," he said. "My dervish has got to dance."

I followed him quiet. We listened when I opened the jail door, but the place was silent as the grave. But from the cell, when we reached it, came a low, whispering sound.

The Governor slipped the trap and looked through.

"All right," he said, and put the key in the door and flung it open.

He were sittin' crouched on the ground, and he looked up at us vacant-like. His face were all fallen down, as it were, and his mouth never ceased to shake and whisper.

The Major shut the door and posted me in a corner. Then he moved to the creature with his whip.

"Up!" he cried. "Up, you dervish, and dance to us!" And he brought the thong with a smack across his shoulders.

The creature leapt under the blow, and then to his feet with a cry, and the Major whipped him till he danced. All round the cell he drove him, lashing and cutting—and again, and many times again, until the poor thing rolled on the floor whimpering and sobbing. I shall have to give an account of this some day. I shall have to whip my master with a red-hot serpent round the blazing furnace of the pit, and I shall do it with agony, because here my love and my obedience was to him.

When it was finished, he bade me put down food and drink that I had brought with me, and come away with him; and we went, leaving him rolling on the floor of the cell, and shut him alone in the empty prison until we should come again at the same time tomorrow.

So day by day this went on, and the dancing three or four times a week, until at last the whip could be left behind, for the man would scream and begin to dance at the mere turning of the key in the lock. And he danced for four months, but not the fifth.

Nobody official came near us all this time. The prison stood lonely as a deserted ruin where dark things have been done.

Once, with fear and trembling, I asked my master how he would account for the inmate of 47 if he was suddenly called upon by authority to open the cell; and he answered, smiling—"I should say it was my mad brother. By his own account, he showed me a brother's love, you know. It would be thought a liberty; but the authorities, I think, would stretch a point for me. But if I got sufficient notice, I should clear out the cell."

I asked him how, with my eyes rather than my lips, and he answered me only with a look.

And all this time he was, outside the prison, living the life of a good man—helping the needy, ministering to the poor. He even entertained occasionally, and had more than one noisy party in his house.

But the fifth month the creature danced no more. He was a dumb, silent animal then, with matted hair and beard; and when one entered he would only look up at one pitifully, as if he said, "My long punishment is nearly ended." How it came that no enquiry was ever made about him I know not, but none ever was.

Perhaps he was one of the wandering gentry that nobody ever knows where they are next. He was unmarried, and had apparently not told of his intended journey to a soul.

And at the last he died in the night. We found him lying stiff and stark in the morning, and scratched with a piece of black crust on a stone of the wall these strange words: "An Eddy on the Floor." Just that—nothing else.

Then the Governor came and looked down, and was silent. Suddenly he caught me by the shoulder.

"Johnson," he cried, "if it was to do again, I would do it! I repent of nothing. But he has paid the penalty, and we call quits. May he rest in peace!"

"Amen!" I answered low. Yet I knew our turn must come for this.

We buried him in quicklime under the wall where the murderers lie, and I made the cell trim and rubbed out the writing, and the Governor locked all up and took away the key. But he locked in more than he bargained for.

For months the place was left to itself, and neither of us went anigh 47. Then one day the workmen was to be put in, and the Major he took me round with him for a last examination of the place before they come.

He hesitated a bit outside a particular cell; but at last he drove in the key and kicked open the door.

"My God!" he says, "he's dancing still!"

My heart was thumpin', I tell you, as I looked over his shoulder. What did we see? What you well understand, sir; but, for all it was no more than that, we knew as well as if it was shouted in our ears that it was him, dancin'. It went round by the walls and drew towards us, and as it stole near I screamed out, "An Eddy on the Floor!" and seized and dragged the Major out and clapped to the door behind us.

"Oh!" I said, "in another moment it would have had us."

He looked at me gloomily.

"Johnson," he said, "I'm not to be frightened or coerced. He may dance, but he shall dance alone. Get a screwdriver and some screws and fasten up this trap. No one from this time looks into this cell."

I did as he bid me, swetin'; and I swear all the time I wrought I dreaded a hand would come through the trap and clutch mine.

On one pretex' or another, from that day till the night you meddled with it, he kep' that cell as close shut as a tomb. And he went his ways, discardin' the past from that time forth. Now and again a over-sensitive

– 105 –

prisoner in the next cell would complain of feelin' uncomfortable. If possible, he would be removed to another; if not, he was dam'd for his fancies. And so it might be goin' on to now, if you hadn't pried and interfered. I don't blame you at this moment, sir. Likely you were an instrument in the hands of Providence; only, as the instrument, you must now take the burden of the truth on your own shoulders. I am a dying man, but I cannot die till I have confessed. Per'aps you may find it in your hart some day to give up a prayer for me—but it must be for the Major as well.

Your obedient servant.

J. Johnson.

WHAT COMMENT OF my own can I append to this wild narrative? Professionally, and apart from personal experiences, I should rule it the composition of an epileptic. That a noted journalist, nameless as he was and is to me, however nomadic in habit, could disappear from human ken, and his fellows rest content to leave him unaccounted for, seems a tax upon credulity so stupendous that I cannot seriously endorse the statement.

Yet, also—there is that little matter of my personal experience.

B ernard Capes was an English writer who published more than 40 books, including romances, ghost stories, poetry, and history. He is best remembered as an accomplished writer of horror stories.

eth's comics and drawings have appeared in the *New York Times*, the *New Yorker*, the *Globe and Mail*, and countless other publications.

His latest graphic novel, *Clyde Fans*, won the prestigious Festival d'Angoulême's Prix Spécial du Jury.

He lives in Guelph, Ontario, with his wife, Tania, in an old house he has named "Inkwell's End."

Publisher's note: "An Eddy on the Floor" was first published in
At a Winter's Fire in 1899 by Doubleday & McClure Company.

Illustrations and design copyright © Seth, 2021

Library and Archives Canada Cataloguing in Publication

Title: An eddy on the floor : a ghost story for Christmas /
Bernard Capes ; designed & decorated by Seth.
Names: Capes, Bernard, 1854-1918, author. |
Seth, 1962- illustrator.
Description: Series statement: Christmas ghost stories
Identifiers: Canadiana 20210214589 |
ISBN 9781771964555 (softcover)
Subjects: LCGFT: Ghost stories. | LCGFT: Christmas fiction.
| LCGFT: Short stories.
Classification: LCC PR6005.A53 E33 2021 |
DDC 823/.912—dc23

Readied for the press by Daniel Wells
Illustrated and designed by Seth
Copy-edited by Meghan Desjardins
Typeset by Christina Angeli

PRINTED AND BOUND IN CANADA